A Kitty Named Indra
Una Gata Llamada Indra

To Todd and Zōsh, my loves and my life.
Para Todd y Zōsh, mis amores y mi vida.

— DLT

To children everywhere, our inspiration and our future.
Para todo los niños, nuestra inspiración y nuestro futuro.

—NPL

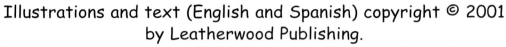
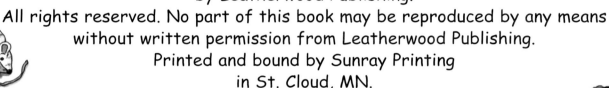

Leatherwood Publishing
20395 County Road 86
Long Prairie, MN 56347

ISBN 0-9741725-0-2

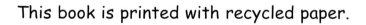

This book is printed with recycled paper.

A Kitty Named Indra
Una Gata Llamada Indra

Written by Dawn Leasman Tanner
Illustrated by Nancy Packard Leasman

Escrito por Dawn Leasman Tanner
Ilustrado por Nancy Packard Leasman

Hello. My name is Indra.

Hola. Mi nombre es Indra.

I live in a house in the city.

Yo vivo en una casa en la ciudad.

The house is all mine,
but I let a few people stay in my house.

La casa es toda mía,
pero yo dejo vivir a unas cuantas personas
en mi casa.

Their names are Michael, Eva and Isabel.

Sus nombres son Miguel, Evita y Isabela.

They keep me company and entertain me.

Ellos me acompañan y me entretienen.

When visitors come to my house,
I sit up high and watch them carefully.

Cuando hay visitantes en mi casa,
yo voy a una posicion alta con mucha atención.

If they are nice,
I might let them play with me.

Si son buenas personas,
tal vez les permita jugar conmigo.

My favorite toy is a stuffed snake
with red, purple and black stripes.

Mi juguete favorito es una culebra de tela
con rayas rojas, moradas y negras.

It crackles when I pounce on it,
and it's filled with catnip.

Cuando me abalanzo sobre ella,
se escucha un crujido,
y está rellena de una hierba gatera.

I can't be bothered to play with ordinary toys;
only the ones good for pouncing and chewing.

Yo no me contento con jugar con juguetes ordinarios;
sólo los que sirven para caer sobre ellos y masticarlos.

I also like to be where my people are.

También me gusta estar donde está mi gente.

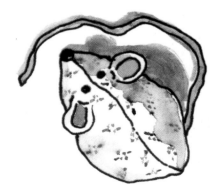

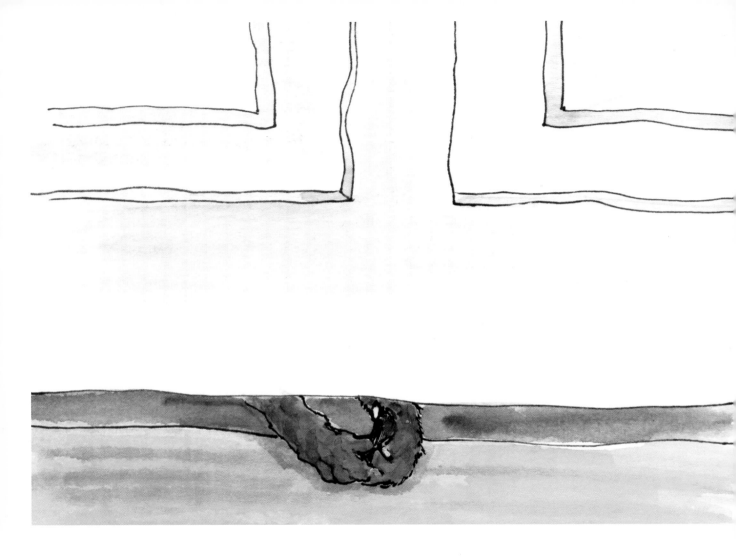

If they shut a door, I meow and pull the door
back and forth with my paw.

Si ellos cierran la puerta,
maúllo y con las patas agito la puerta.

This makes noise so I can get in.

Ésto hace ruido y de ésta forma puedo entrar.

On Sunday mornings, my people sleep in.
I pounce on them in bed
and drop toys by their heads.

Los domingos por la mañana, mi gente duerme un poco más
y yo salto encima de ellos en la cama
y dejo caer juguetes cerca de sus cabezas.

This gets their attention so we can play fetch.

Ésto atrae su atención y entonces jugamos
a buscar y traer cosas.

I'd throw my toys for them,
but they are much too slow.

Yo tiraría mis juguetes para ellos,
pero ellos son demasiado lentos.

My favorite food is tuna fish.
I'll be nice to anybody who will share their tuna with me.

Mi comida favorita es atún.
Seré muy buena con quién comparta su atún conmigo.

I don't like to share,
but I like my people to share with me.

A mí no me gusta compartir, pero sí me gusta
que mi gente comparta lo suyo conmigo.

Yes, I'm a bit spoiled, but I love me that way...
because I'm a kitty named Indra, and this is my house.

Sí, soy un poco mimado, pero me amo de ésta forma...
porque yo soy una gata llamada Indra, y ésta es mi casa.

Special thanks to: Indra, the self-possessed cat;
Javier Martinez; the Long Prairie Hispanic Liaison
Office; James Mayer, Ph.D., Academy Mayer
Language Center; and the West 7th Community
and Family Centers.